Supervillain of the Day

SUPERVILLAIN
OF THE DAY

SUPERVILLAIN
OF THE DAY

by Katie Lynn Daniels

Cover design by Jordan Miller
Interior formatting by Aubrey Hansen

Special thanks to Elizabeth Kirkwood for reading absolutely
everything I sent her, however meaningless; to Jordan Miller for his
brilliant cover designs; to Evening L. Aspen for her meticulous
editing; to Aubrey Hansen for helping clueless me with formatting;
to Elizabeth Liberty for last minute test reading and her brilliant
insight; to Lady Elanor for her brit picking; to Jordan Smith for
introducing me to Jordan and for his support of my series; and to
Jordan for his encouragement and scrutiny of my portrayal of
London.

Published by:
Provide Your Own – Books
PO Box 748
Tompkinsville, KY 42167
Website: Books.ProvideYourOwn.com

Print Edition, January 2013
ISBN-13: 978-0615742878 (Provide Your Own - Books)
ISBN-10: 0615742874
Library of Congress Control Number: 2012923999

This is a work of fiction. Any similarities to real people, living or
dead, are merely coincidental.

To Rick
Because you believed in me
Because you were my hero

TABLE OF CONTENTS

THE ANNOYING JOURNALIST

No one knew that the new mayor was a supervillain until the day he lost his temper with his secretary and tried to force-choke her from across the room.

But then, no one knew that the mayor's secretary was a supervillain until the mayor tried to force-choke her. The resulting battle lasted for six hours and destroyed the court house, as well as much of the surrounding area.

That was the first outbreak, and soon it became clear that the phenomena was not restricted to one city alone. An epidemic had broken out all over the world and was quickly becoming uncontrollable. Many victims sought out medical advice, but there was little conventional doctors could do. Symptoms included superhuman abilities, mental deterioration, and strong inclination towards violence and chaos.

During the first two weeks of the outbreak, reactions from the ordinary inhabitants of the planet spanned from disbelief to panic. Once it had been unalterably established that supervillains did exist and were taking over the world, the panic changed to a kind of incessant demand that someone do something about the problem. No one knew what to do and so, as a general rule, nothing was done.

There was no way to cure the supervillains, no way to contain them, and rarely was there any way to kill them. The initial reaction of the public was to scream for a superhero. Many tried to oblige, but none were successful. Those with superpowers either went insane or succumbed to the dark side. Those without were ineffective. Scientists worked with medical practitioners to try to artificially create superpowers without the unwanted side effects, but their attempts were disastrous. Some of the worst villains came out of laboratories, although most of the experiments resulted in horrible deaths for the would-be superhero volunteers.

At last the population of planet Earth simply gave up. They settled down to live their lives, making minor adjustments to accommodate their superhuman neighbors, and hoping the phenomena would die out eventually and the world would go back to normal.

Those lucky few who were fortunate enough not to be affected by the supervillains flaunted their good fortune and laughed at the rest of the world. One of the most notable villain-free zones was London, England. They declared that the peacefulness of their streets was a sign that they were indeed the greatest city in the world.

However, not everyone was as grateful for London's reprieve as they should have been. In fact, for the editor of the London Star, the lack of supervillains was an intolerable situation. The London Star was a tabloid paper specializing in stories of the paranormal and supernatural, and what could be more of both than supervillains?

Mr. Stephen Hendrick, known to his friends as Steve, was fifty-six years of age and should have, in his opinion, retired six years ago. He hated newspapers almost as much as he loved them. He despised people. He believed in nothing. His personal opinion of the world was that the entire thing was a giant hoax. He delighted in telling the biggest and most elaborate lies to his audience to see how many believed them, thus proving how gullible most people were. Anything remotely plausible was never printed in his paper.

He had a face that could be described as red and jovial, without the jovial. He was short and round and wrinkled – somewhat like a slug. When he wasn't shouting at his employees he was shouting at his friends, his wife, inanimate objects, or at total strangers. At the moment, he was trying to explain the situation, very patiently, to one of his lead reporters who simply failed to see the point.

"I'm as unhappy about the lack of supervillains as you are," the reporter said. He went by his last name, which was Floyd. His first name was Jeffry and as a general rule he ignored this fact. He sat on Mr. Hendrick's desk and swung his legs back and forth as he talked, happily oblivious to the fact that the reason he was able to swing them was because they weren't long enough to reach the floor. "In fact, I have much better reasons to be unhappy about it then you do. But the facts are simple—there aren't any supervillains. So we'll just have to wait until there are."

"It's been six weeks," Mr. Hendrick growled. "And not a villain to be seen. I want to know why."

"Many people do, sir," Floyd said.

"I want you to find out why," Mr. Hendrick said. "I want a supervillain story by next week."

"Wait a minute," Floyd said uneasily. "You want me to find out why there are no supervillains or you want me to find a supervillain?"

"Yes," Mr. Hendrick said. "Get to it."

Floyd laughed. "I don't think you understand. The two are mutually exclusive."

"Find a conspiracy theory. I don't care. Just get me a supervillain story."

"And what if there truly aren't any villains in England?"

"Invent one. It's what you do best."

"And I only have a week?"

"That's what I said."

"Give me two weeks," Floyd begged.

"You can go," Mr. Hendrick told him.

"Suppose I can't find one..." Floyd said tentatively.

"Find some," Mr. Hendrick threatened.

"Or?" Floyd raised one eyebrow in disbelief.

"Or else!" Mr. Hendrick roared. "Now get out of this office and don't come back without my story!"

Floyd lost no time in obeying.

"What's the matter, Floyd?

The clerk at the front desk was a bright girl named Mary Margaret. She had bleached blond hair and wore too much lipstick. Floyd's steps slowed as he passed her desk and he glanced at her warily.

"Are you in trouble for bringing competitors papers to work again?" she asked.

"The Times is not a competitor to this paper," Floyd said. "And you know it."

"But Mr. Hendrick doesn't like it, does he?" she said with a smirk.

"You do," Floyd accused. "You steal my paper."

Mary raised her eyebrows. "You have no evidence of that," she said crisply.

"Yet," Floyd threatened. "I have no evidence yet. And when I do..."

"You'll do what?" she teased. "You know Mr. Hendrick will be more angry that you brought it in then about me stealing it."

"Know-it-all," Floyd retorted. "I have work to do."

"Oh yes, I know what Mr. Hendrick wanted," she said, running her fingers over the desk. "You're supposed to get a supervillain story."

"Yeah, and I've only got a week to do it," Floyd said. "Goodbye."

"Everyone else in this office likes my company," Mary said, pouting. "Everyone but you."

"You steal my newspapers!" Floyd exclaimed.

"I could give it back," Mary offered, reaching under her desk.

"In exchange for what?" Floyd said suspiciously.

"Give me your opinion on this," she said.

She folded the paper open and smoothed the page. "Supervillain attacks escalate in the US," she read aloud. "Superhero initiative still an option."

"Which is absolute rubbish," Floyd said heatedly.

"What?" Mary Margaret asked casually. "The supervillains or the superheroes?"

"The superheroes," Floyd said. "There is no such thing."

"As though you know," she laughed at him.

"I do know," he said, his brows narrowing in irritation.

"You are the only person in the world who refuses to believe in superheroes as though it's an already established scientific fact," she said, still laughing.

"Can I have the paper now, please?" he asked patiently.

"You said please!" she said in mock amazement. "I thought you didn't understand how to use that word!"

Floyd tried to snatch the paper from her but she was faster.

"That's it!" Floyd said. "I will never trust you again!"

"You don't trust me anyway," she retorted.

Floyd started to answer and then changed his mind, turning to leave.

"Where are you going?" Mary Margaret called after him.

"Scotland Yard, if it's any of your business," Floyd answered.

"Trying to get yourself arrested?" she taunted.

Floyd ignored her.

....

8

The brain center for crime fighting in London is Scotland Yard, or New Scotland Yard as it is more properly called. Many unfortunate souls have asked about Old Scotland Yard only to discover it never really existed. How you can have a New Scotland Yard without an Old Scotland Yard is a riddle with an answer of such great complexity that those who seek after it usually give up their quest for knowledge in favor of escaping with their wits intact.

"Excuse me, can I help you?"

The clerk who addressed Floyd looked like he'd just barely grown out of the teenager stage, but he spoke with all the confidence his surroundings imparted to him.

"My name is Jeffry Floyd," Floyd said. "I'm a reporter for the London Star and I'm researching supervillain activity in the area."

The young clerk blinked. "There is no supervillain activity in the area," he said.

Floyd smiled. "I know. That's what I'm investigating."

"Um, okay," the young man said. "What would you like to know?"

"How many unsolved cases in the last six weeks do you have involving assault or vandalism?"

The clerk blinked again. "I don't know," he stammered. "I don't have access to that kind of information."

"Then I suggest you let me talk to someone who does," Floyd said confidently.

The young man hemmed and hawed for a moment. "Wait right here," he said finally, and disappeared into the maze behind him.

Floyd waited.

The officer who followed the clerk back into the lobby was tall and confident, with piercing blue eyes that missed nothing.

"Can I help you?" he asked crisply.

"My name is Jeffry Floyd," Floyd repeated, feeling suddenly less sure of himself. "I'm a reporter for the London Star and I'm researching the lack of supervillain activity in the area."

"What kind of research?" the officer asked.

"Why there isn't any," Floyd said, attempting a disarming smile.

It didn't work.

"Are you sure you're not trying to prove that there *are* supervillains?" the policeman said.

Floyd was startled. "I beg your pardon?"

"I'm familiar with your paper," he said impatiently. "I think you'd be more interested in proving that there are supervillains and that the apparent lack of them is a cover-up than you would be in writing some glorious piece about why there aren't any."

This was the truth, and it left Floyd scrambling for a new cover story.

"You're a terrible liar, Mr. Floyd," the officer said. "You can go now."

"No, wait!" Floyd said desperately. "Hear me out. I have a theory."

"Every crackpot reporter has a theory," the officer said patiently.

"Either there's a reason for it or there's not," Floyd said. "If there is then I'll find it, but right now there doesn't appear to be any reason at all. And if that's the case then doesn't it seem more likely that there are supervillains and they're hiding themselves for a darker, more sinister purpose? And if they are, wouldn't it be better for us to find them out before they're ready and foil their evil plan?"

The officer pondered for a moment. "What makes you qualified to find this reason?" he asked.

"I know what I'm talking about," Floyd retorted.

"I think you sound like you've been reading too many comic books."

"Perhaps I have," Floyd admitted, "But it doesn't change that I know what I'm talking about."

"From reading comic books?"

"No! I'm..." he floundered.

"Obsessed," the policeman offered dryly.

Floyd shrugged.

"All right," the officer said finally. "You may be on to something. We can't officially investigate, of course, but if you turn up something, it could be very beneficial."

"You'll help?" Floyd stammered in amazement.

"I'll give you a file," the sergeant corrected. "One file. Under one condition."

"What's that?"

"You tell me anything you find out," the officer said, "And you let me approve anything you write before it's published. I don't want any mention of the police in that tabloid of yours."

"Not a problem," Floyd said earnestly. "Thank you."

"I'll have Bernard print off the file for you," the policeman said. "And here's my card. Call me if you find anything."

The name on the card was Sergeant Joseph S. Adams.

Floyd glanced at it and put it in his pocket.

"Thank you," he said again. "You've been very helpful."

"And if you double cross me," Sergeant Adams warned, "I will find something to arrest you for."

"I believe it," Floyd said fervently. "I'll be in touch."

THE SKEPTICAL POLICEMAN

Sergeant Adams was the sort of man who did not read the kind of papers Floyd wrote for. He was serious, sober, hard-working, dependable, and sensible. He wasn't sure which bothered him more—not knowing what was going on with the supervillains or letting a no-good reporter find out that information for him.

The file he had given Floyd detailed an incident that had occurred six weeks ago, the day after the very first supervillain report had come in from the US. Two squad cars carrying four officers had replied to a distress call. The official story was that two thugs had been abusing a young girl. The facts didn't agree with the official story.

No one had died that night, amazingly, but they were all in the hospital afterwards, some with more bruises than others. The thugs had escaped, along with whatever it was that had enabled them to take down four trained officers without leaving a mark behind.

Floyd betook himself to the area with alacrity. The trail was long cold, but that didn't keep him from standing in the alley staring at the surrounding buildings, looking for marks or scratches, and standing on the roof of said buildings staring down at the pavement as though the answer would be written on it. The inhabitants subjected to his scrutiny either glared at him and shut their windows, or opened their windows and shouted at him. He ignored both types.

Standing on firm ground, he attempted to playact the events of that night, reconstructed from police report in his hand.

Imagining he was with the thugs he spun around, picked a direction and ran. The tenants decided that as long as he was gone there was no point in calling the police to pick him up.

Floyd came out suddenly onto a busy street and looked both ways, realizing that at this point he'd lost his imaginary prey.

Sticking his hands deep in his pockets he trudged back in the direction he'd come from. He was almost back to where he'd begun when a new thought struck him, and he started back towards Scotland Yard.

....

"Can I help you?" the clerk asked without even looking up. It was much later in the day, and the young man had been replaced by a young woman with dark hair that kept falling in her eyes.

14

"I'd like to talk to Sergeant Adams, please," Floyd said, trying to sound as though he knew exactly what he was doing.

"Is he expecting you?"

"He should be."

"What's your name?"

"Floyd."

The clerk looked up at him and blinked once.

"Jeffry Floyd," he hastily corrected.

"Just a moment please," the clerk said smoothly. Floyd resisted the urge to pace.

Five minutes later, the lanky form of Joseph Adams came strolling out of the bowels of the police station.

"That was quick," he observed. "Do you have something to report?"

"I may be onto something," Floyd said excitedly. "But I need more information."

Adams frowned. "I don't like the sound of that."

"I can explain," Floyd said quickly. "I have a theory."

"I've heard this one before."

"Listen," Floyd said. "I went to the scene of the crime. I looked for evidence of supervillain activity."

"It's been six weeks," Adams interjected. "I think any evidence would be gone by now."

"That's possible," Floyd agreed, "so if you have photographs from that night I'd like to see them. But there actually was quite a bit of information left in the landscape itself that was able to give me an idea of what kind of villain might have done it."

"You've already decided there's a villain?" Adams said. "Based on one report?"

"I can't say for sure," Floyd said warily.

"I told you I'm not interested in proving the existence of supervillains in this city," Adams said, his voice thick with disapproval.

"I told you I would investigate and tell you what I found," Floyd said defensively. "And I'm telling you that I found something but the evidence is non-conclusive."

"I think you're lying!" Adams shouted. Everyone in the lobby stopped what they were doing and looked at him in surprise. A door opened and an official head looked out.

"Is there a problem?" the owner of the head asked.

"No," Adams said, flushing. "I was just leaving. Come on, Floyd. We're going to get some dinner."

....

The restaurant Adams chose was small and quiet. It was almost dark by the time they actually reached it and Floyd was growing increasingly annoyed. Still the policeman made him wait until after they'd been seated, at a table by a window, and placed their orders.

"I don't want to eat," Floyd said impatiently. "I want to talk."

"So talk," Adams said, folding his hands. "But let me say something first."

Floyd waited.

"You need my help?" the policeman queried.

"I need data," Floyd said. "Scotland Yard has that data."

"I'm willing to listen to you," Adams said. "You make an odd kind of sense, but I remain skeptical. So here's the deal. You have half an hour. In that amount of time you convince me that there is something worth investigating and I'll help you. If you can't impress me then I never want to see your face again, understand?"

"Fine," Floyd said confidently. He turned on his camera and started looking through the photos.

"You took pictures?" Adams said in surprise.

"Of course I did," Floyd said. "I'm a journalist. It's what I do. Actually," he added, "I'm a photographer. I only do the journaling part because they make me."

He turned the camera around and showed Adams.

"It's a dumpster," Adams commented.

"See the dent?"

"Yeah, I see it."

"What do you think would make a dent like that?"

Adams shrugged. "The truck that empties the dumpster?"

"Wrong," Floyd said with a grin. "The truck picks it up from the side. There's no way it could make a dent on the top like that, not even by accident."

"So... something fell on it?" the sergeant guessed.

"Right!" Floyd said, taking the camera back. "There's just one problem. Whatever "it" was would have to be very heavy to dent one inch steel like that. And there's simply nothing that heavy in the vicinity."

"Maybe it was dented while it was being used in another area," Adams said.

"Maybe," Floyd agreed. "And if I can talk to the company who owns it I might be able to find out. Or if you had any photos from the area prior to the accident that would also offer conclusive proof."

"Proof of what?" Adams said, puzzled.

"Proof of whether that dent is the result of something heavy falling on it, or being smashed by a superhuman," Floyd said.

"You're trying to prove that there's a supervillain loose in the streets of London by pointing out a dent on a dumpster?"

"It's not conclusive," Floyd said, showing a flash of irritation. "I told you that already. But it's not all I have."

He showed Adams another picture.

"It's a crack," Adams said, stating the obvious.

"Use your imagination," Floyd suggested.

"All right," Adams said in exasperation. "It's a crack that could be perceived as being in the shape of a giant footprint."

"Exactly," Floyd said triumphantly, retrieving his camera and putting it away.

"That doesn't prove anything," Adams added.

"I'm not trying to prove anything," Floyd said. "I know the difference between proof and conjecture. If this were proof we wouldn't be having this conversation."

"Than what are you trying to say?"

Floyd leaned forward and put his fingers together. "I'm trying to say that I cannot prove or disprove the existence of a supervillain based on this evidence," he said. "Certain signs seem to indicate that on exists, but they could be easily explained away by other means. The data is

18

inconclusive. You need to give me more case files."

"So you can gather more data," Adams clarified.

"And form a bigger picture," Floyd agreed.

Adams pondered, and this time Floyd was content to wait.

"I don't trust you," the policeman said finally. "But for a low-grade journalist, you make a frightening amount of sense."

"You'll help me?" Floyd said eagerly.

"Same terms as before," Adams warned. "I'll give you more files, and you bring anything you find to me."

"Agreed," Floyd said instantly, standing and reaching for his coat.

"Where are you going?" Adams asked.

"I've got work to do," Floyd said. "Can you call your office and have those files waiting for me, please?"

"I suppose," Adams said, caught off-guard. "Don't you sleep?"

"Sleep?" Floyd said with a grin. "Who needs sleep? I'll see you tomorrow, officer."

THE DEAD POLITICIAN

Sleep was exactly what Floyd did not do. He spent the night running around doing as easily in the dark what he had in the daylight: annoying citizens, snapping pictures, and looking for clues that didn't really constitute as evidence.

But when it came to knocking on doors and asking people specific questions he hesitated. He wasn't in the habit of asking permission to execute his usually hair-brained schemes, but then again, he wasn't in the habit of asking the police for help either.

It was four in the morning when he returned to Scotland Yard, and he wasn't overly surprised to find out that Sergeant Adams wasn't there. He borrowed a flash drive from the clerk, copied his pictures onto it, and left it with specific instructions that it should be given to Adams as soon as he came in. Then he went home.

Home was a tiny, dingy flat on the third floor of a building that looked like it had been built in the dark ages. The stairs creaked in protest, and even under his slight weight they felt like they would give way at any moment. The door stuck. The lock didn't work. And the lights came on with hesitancy, as though reluctant to see the interior of the room.

If they were reluctant, it was with good reason. The room was a mess. The sink was stacked with unwashed dishes. A card table was balanced on old magazines to stay level and was covered with ancient newspapers and cheap paperback novels. Most of the light bulbs in the room had burnt out and hadn't been replaced. The windows needed washing. A thick layer of dust covered the furniture. Between the poor lighting and the dust there was no way to discern the color of anything.

Floyd was practiced at ignoring the dust. He showered, went to bed, and woke up four hours later. He checked his mail, threw most of it away, checked his email, and then went back to the police station.

He bumped into Adams in the lobby.

"Oh good, you're here," he said. "Did you see the pictures I left you?"

"I just got in," Adams replied. "But let me guess. You have more inconclusive evidence."

"Exactly," Floyd said. "But the amount of inconclusive evidence is accumulating."

"What does that mean?"

Floyd hesitated, trying to figure out how to word his request.

"I want to try to find some witnesses," he said slowly. "But I wanted to check with you before I did it."

"And what does that mean?"

Floyd flicked through the pictures and pointed one out. "I want to knock on every door on this street," he said, "And ask the people who live there what they saw the night the incident was reported."

"Which case is this?" Adams asked.

Floyd handed over the folder. "It was just last week," he said. "They'll remember that."

Adams flicked through the papers. "We already questioned everyone," he said. "Their statements are in here."

"I want to talk to them in person," Floyd said. "It could make a difference. I would say I'm from the paper. I wouldn't involve the police at all."

"Then why are you bothering to ask me?" Adams asked, puzzled.

"Because," Floyd said earnestly, "I do need your help, and I can't afford to lose your goodwill because I did something you didn't approve of."

"That's commendable," Adams said. "Sure. You can get eyewitness testimony. Just keep the police out of it."

"Thanks," Floyd said. "I'll let you know what I find."

"You'd better," the policeman retorted. "And Floyd?"

"Yes?" Floyd paused, alerted by his tone of voice.

"I want to run a background check on you," Adams said. "I thought I'd warn you."

"I'd rather you not," Floyd said warily.

"Why is that?" Adams asked. "Have you got something to hide?"

"Of course," he said candidly. "Hasn't everyone?"

"What am I going to find, Floyd?" Adams asked. "What did you do?"

"It's more like what I haven't done," Floyd hedged. "And anyway, I'm going to go get to work on this. Have fun with your background thingy."

He backed slowly towards the door, then turned and ran like the police were on his heels.

....

The first door opened on a huge man who simply stared as Floyd rattled off his credentials, his reasons for being there, and his requests for information. When he stopped talking the man didn't answer, and after a long, awkward pause he shut the door. Floyd decided against knocking again.

The second door was opened by a middle aged woman in a business suit who cut him off before he'd had a chance to get a word out and told him flatly that they weren't interested. When Floyd tried to explain, she lost her temper and screamed a string of language that made even him feel daunted and he scurried away quickly.

The third door was opened by a sixteen-year-old girl. Her blond hair was in pigtails and her right arm was in a sling. Floyd had become wary of people who opened doors, so he didn't say anything right away, and waited to see how she would react.

"Can I help you?" she prompted.

"Oh, yes!" Floyd said, startled. "My name is Floyd. I'm a reporter for the London Star. I'm investigating reports of supervillains in the area."

To his amazement, the girl burst into tears. She stepped out of the building, pulled the door closed behind her, and sat down on the stoop and cried. After an awkward moment of not knowing what to do, Floyd sat next to her in companionable silence and waited.

"He did this to me," she said finally, between hiccuping sobs. She gestured to her broken arm. "No one believed me. They told me I was stressed and imagining things. But I know what I saw, mister. And it was horrible..."

Floyd patted her shoulder reassuringly and kept waiting.

The girl drew a shuddering breath and seemed to recover herself. "It was huge," she said. "It was...well, it was dark. I couldn't see it very well. But it was at least as tall as a building. That's when I knew that... that it couldn't be human."

"What's your name?" Floyd asked.

"Lisa," she said. "And you are..."

"Floyd," he repeated. "When did this happen, Lisa?"

"Yesterday," she said promptly.

"Yesterday?" Floyd repeated in amazement. "Here?"

"No," she shook her head. "Uptown. I was watching the parade."

"What parade?"

She stared at him like he wasn't human anymore. "Where do you live?" she asked. "The New Year's Day Parade, of course."

"Um," Floyd said, running his fingers through his hair. "Can you show me?"

She nodded eagerly. "I can't believe someone actually believes me," she said, laughing nervously. "Everyone thought I was nuts when I wouldn't stop talking about it."

"I believe you," Floyd said, helping her up. "There's no doubt about that."

She flashed a smile and then glanced down at her stockinged feet. "Let me get my shoes on," she said, "And tell my mum where I'm going. I'll be back in a jiffy."

"I'll be waiting right here," Floyd promised.

In scarcely two minutes she was back out. There was no sign that she'd been crying, and her face was wearing a sunny smile that affected the entire street. Floyd grinned just looking at her.

"Let's go," she said eagerly.

They walked half a mile, caught a bus, and finally found themselves near Piccadilly.

"This is a pretty nice part of town for random thugs to be doing over," Floyd said, looking around appreciatively.

"Come on," Lisa grabbed his hand and pulled him along.

They stopped abruptly on the sidewalk. "It was here," Lisa said.

"Here?" Floyd questioned.

"Right here."

"With people around?"

"No," she shook her head. "I was late coming home. The streets were deserted."

Floyd sighed and glanced around. There was a steady flow of traffic on the street. People hurried back and forth on the sidewalk.

"Tell me exactly what happened."

"I was walking home—"

"What time was this?"

"After midnight sometime. I'm not sure."

"Alone?"

"Yes."

Floyd shook his head. "You're lying," he said.

26

"Excuse me?"

"Lying," Floyd repeated. "This place is never deserted, especially not on New Year's Day. So where were you, really?"

"None of your business," Lisa said uneasily.

"Then you're absolutely no help," Floyd snapped.

"All right, all right," she said, twisting a strand of hair around her finger nervously. "Just don't tell my mum, all right? I was supposed to meet my boyfriend in the park."

"This park?" Floyd pointed across the street. Lisa nodded.

"You were walking through Hyde Park, after dark, alone?"

She nodded again.

"Did your boyfriend ever turn up?"

She shook her head.

Floyd sighed. "What happened?"

"There was a horrible rumbling noise. I looked behind me and saw this... this thing. It was as tall as a building. I couldn't make out anything distinct because it was taller than the street lights. The ground shook with every step it took."

"Okay," Floyd said. "What did you do?"

"I ran," she continued. "I was terrified. I ran as fast as I could but even walking the... the thing was faster."

"And what did he do?"

"He just brushed me out of the way," she shuddered. "It's all kind of a blur, but I know I was flying through the air, and then I hit the pavement and... and I think I blacked out because the next thing I knew I woke up in the hospital and no one believed me when I told them what happened."

"Hmmm," Floyd said thoughtfully. "And this was after the parade?"

"That's right."

"I'm going up on the roof," Floyd said. "Wait here."

"The roof?" Lisa asked, confused. "Why..."

Floyd was already climbing up the fire escape on the side of the building. She watched in increasing confusion as he made his way to the top.

"Where does the parade end?" he shouted down.

"Parliament Square," she said. "You really don't know this?"

"Well," Floyd said thoughtfully, and climbed down.

"Let's go take a look," he said, reappearing on the street.

"A look at what?"

"I don't know," Floyd said. "I'm following a hunch."

Lisa followed him as they walked to Parliament Square and beyond, rambling through a maze of streets, dodging traffic and pedestrians alike.

"Who are you, really?" she asked.

"I told you," Floyd said. "I'm a reporter for the London Star."

"And you're doing a story about supervillains?"

"If I can find one, yes. Oh!"

Catching sight of something, he dashed down the sidewalk towards Westminster Bridge, and Lisa had to run to keep up.

"What is it?" she asked, when they finally slowed to a stop.

"This!" Floyd said triumphantly. Yellow tape surrounded the sidewalk where a large piece of the railing was missing, crumbled somewhere in the dark river below. "What happened here?"

"Oh, I think I saw that in the paper this morning," Lisa said. "Some politician drove off the bridge last night."

Floyd stared. "You don't just drive off this bridge," he said. "Have you looked at this railing?"

Lisa shrugged.

"The monster didn't want to kill you," Floyd mused, staring at the rubble. "He just brushed you out of the way to get to another target. This target."

Lisa's eyes widened. "What are you going to do?" she asked.

"I think I'm going to go to the police," Floyd said.

"Will they listen to you?"

He sighed. "Probably not. But I'm going to go to them anyway."

Supervillain of the Day

THE SHORT-LIVED BREAKUP

Floyd returned to Scotland Yard shortly after lunch time, brandishing a copy of the Times like a war trophy.

Adams eyes widened when he saw him.

"You get more done in four hours then six patrolmen get done in an entire day," he said.

Floyd grinned. "I found a witness," he said. "Sixteen year old girl with a broken arm."

Adams frowned. "That wasn't in the report," he said.

"That's because it didn't happen the night the disturbance was reported," he said. "It happened yesterday."

"Yesterday?"

"Yeah." Floyd spread out a paper on top of Adams' lunch. "What can you tell me about this guy?"

Adams looked at it. "What do you want to know?" he asked slowly.

"Anything," Floyd said. "Anything that isn't in that paper."

"No," Adams said in a voice that brooked no argument.

Floyd argued.

"All I need is a little information," he pleaded. "Something that wasn't in the official report."

"We don't leave things out of the official report."

"What about the guardrail?" Floyd asked.

"What?"

"The guardrail," Floyd repeated. "How did a car go through that anyway?"

"It went over the rail."

"That's not what the official report says," Floyd grinned triumphantly.

"Have you seen the official report?" Adams challenged.

Floyd looked crestfallen. "No," he admitted, then smiled slyly. "Yet," he added.

"You know what?" Adams said, folding up the paper and shoving it under his desk. "I think we're done here."

"What?" Floyd exclaimed, surprised and crestfallen at the same time.

"I should have known," Adams said. "All you care about is a sensational story, and I'm not going to be involved with that."

"What? No! This is connected to the supervillain investigation."

"You can't prove that," Adams said. "This is a high profile case that I'm sure a paper like yours would love to smear with their dirty hands. Now get out."

"No, no, no!" Floyd said desperately. "Listen. There is a villain in London. The eyewitness proves it. She described the creature that attacked her and the description fits with the damage seen in those photos. There's no denying it anymore— the villains are real, and they're here."

"Congratulations," Adams said. "You have your story. Now get out before I throw you out."

"I don't have anything!" Floyd shouted. "Supervillains are everywhere. They've taken over the world. There's nothing unusual in that."

"So?"

"So why does it take two days of detective work to prove that there are any in London?" Floyd said. "Why are they hiding? What are they up to? Who are they working for? There's a sinister plan here, Sergeant, and the only way to prevent it from being carried out is to guess what it is and make the first strike."

"You said that when we met yesterday," Adams said. "I'm not convinced."

"You listened to me then," Floyd pointed out.

"You were just a crack-pot reporter then," Adams said. "Now you're a potential threat. This conversation is over."

"A threat?" Floyd repeated incredulously. "We're on the same side here!"

"Are we?"Adams demanded, whirling on him. "Who do you really work for, Floyd?"

Floyd stopped talking abruptly.

"I thought so," Adams said bitterly. "Get out of here before I have you arrested."

"Joseph," Floyd said, confused, pleading.

"I did a background check on you, Floyd!" Adams exclaimed, his rage revealing his sense of betrayal. "Do you want to know what I found? Nothing. As far as the records can show you don't exist. Is Jeffry Floyd even your real name?"

"I..." Floyd started to protest and changed his mind. "No."

"Are you even from this country?"

"I..."

"Nevermind," Adams said quickly. "I don't want to know. Just get out of here before I change my mind about letting you go."

Floyd didn't move, his eyes locked on Adams', still pleading.

"Now!" The police officer shouted.

"I'm sorry," Floyd said softly. He started to say something else and changed his mind.

"I'm sorry," he repeated, and then he was gone.

....

Humans are very adaptable creatures, quickly becoming accustomed to the strangest of occurrences if they happen frequently enough. Floyd's first appearance at Scotland Yard was met with suspicion and distrust, but by the time he arrived for the fourth time he was greeted with no more than a nod from the clerk on duty as he found his own way back to Adams' space.

There were few people in the building at this hour, and many of the lights had been shut down in unused offices to conserve power. Floyd looked around surreptitiously before slipping behind Adams desk without turning on the light. The computer screen lit up with a dull glow, but it would hopefully attract less attention than the overhead light would.

He waited impatiently as the screen booted up, trying to resist the urge to look back over his shoulder. There was no reason for Adams to be here this late at night, and no reason anyone else would come poking around. If they did he could just say he had come to leave a report. He hoped they would believe that or, better yet, just not come poking around.

He got the correct password on his third try, cursed his stupidity, and searched the system for the data he'd requested earlier in the day. He was astounded by the number of results. The violence had spreader faster than he'd even guessed and it seemed like the police were doing absolutely nothing. He inserted the flash drive he'd brought along and copied the data as quickly as possible, hoping desperately that it wouldn't set off some alarm he didn't know about. He knew that what he was doing was stupid, very stupid, but after Adams' dismissal earlier that day he didn't have any choice.

To his relief the copying finished without incident. He disconnected the flash drive, logged out the system, and powered down the computer. He started towards the doorway and bumped straight into someone.

One vise-like hand gripped his collar and the overhead lights flickered on. Floyd stared up in terror at Sergeant Adams.

"I can explain!" he said hastily, knowing that it was a complete lie.

"You'd better explain!" Adams exclaimed. "What do you think you're doing?"

He saw the flash drive Floyd was still holding and wrested it from his grip.

"What's on here?" He asked, holding it up. "What were you stealing?"

"Nothing!" Floyd stammered. "It was just something I was leaving for you..."

He faltered under the steely gaze of the policeman, knowing full well that Adams could see straight through his intentions.

"It's the reports you wouldn't give me this afternoon," he confessed.

"How did you get in the system?" Adams demanded.

Floyd shrugged. "I'm good with computers."

"You're good with computers?" he exclaimed. "That's government data! You could go to prison for twenty years for this!"

"Please don't do that," Floyd begged, cowering away from him. "Please."

"Give me one good reason not to," Adams said. "One reason!"

Floyd faltered. Adams swore and turned away.

"Because!" Floyd shouted desperately. "Because I'm the only one who can stop the supervillains from taking over this city."

Something in his tone made the sergeant turn back.

"You?" Adams said. "Why you?"

"I... I know more about supervillains than anyone else," Floyd stammered, trying to be honest without giving away the truth.

"The attack didn't even happen until six weeks ago!" Adams retorted. "How can you be an expert about something that barely exists?"

Floyd hesitated.

"Tell me!"

"I just know!" Floyd said. "You have to trust me!"

"I don't trust you," Adams said angrily, holding up the flash drive for proof. "I can't."

"Is that true?" Floyd asked. "Or is it just because protocol demands that you don't?"

For once it was Adams who had to think about the reply, and Floyd dared to hope.

"I know you," Adams replied finally. "And I know your type. You'll say anything, do anything, just to get a good scandal to shock the public with."

"You think I'm doing this for the story?" Floyd exclaimed.

"You're a reporter, Floyd," Adams said wearily. "I shouldn't have to tell you this."

"This is way bigger then just one news story."

"Why else would you be doing it?"

"Because," Floyd floundered. "Because it's the right thing to do. Because if I don't a whole lot of people are going to get hurt."

Adams paused.

Floyd waited.

"Will you help me?" he asked finally.

"You could be lying," Adams admitted.

"But I'm not," Floyd said. "You know when I'm lying, and I'm not. Look at me! I'm telling you the truth."

His eyes were wide, panicking, and darker in color than Adams remembered them.

"You're telling the truth," Adams said. Floyd let out his breath and sagged against the wall in relief.

"But I don't trust you," Adams added.

Floyd tensed again.

"Then what?" he asked. "Where does that leave us?"

Adams looked at the flash drive and sighed, then placed it in Floyd's hand.

"Go home," he said.

"What?"

"Go home," Adams repeated. "You were never here, we never spoke; I never gave you any reports."

Floyd's fingers closed over the drive. "I don't understand," he said finally.

"You'll figure it out," Adams told him. "Now go."

THE DETECTIVE REPORTER 5

The cat in parliament square didn't understand the actions of the person who was failing to pay attention to it.

"If you're going to put up a fuss," Floyd told it, "You could at least say something useful."

The cat stopped prowling and mewed piteously.

"Yeah," Floyd responded. "I know. But I'm trying to think here."

One velvety paw batted at his shoe. Floyd sighed and crouched down to pet it.

He glanced up and continued to scan his surroundings, hoping they would reveal some clue even though he'd seen them a dozen times already.

"Do you want to help?" Floyd asked the cat. It walked back and forth under his hand, purring loudly. Floyd sighed again.

"I know," he murmured. "But there's a whole world out there that needs saving. We're the only ones who stand between them and utter chaos... well, not us," he said finally. "Me."

He looked at the printed photographs in his hand, a small sampling of the dozens he carried in a bag slung over his shoulder.

"It could be nothing," he admitted to the cat. "It could be nothing at all. I could be chasing shadows. But honestly, isn't that better than not chasing at all? I'd rather be wrong than right I guess..."

"Hey mister!" A child's voice piped up. "Are you crazy?"

Floyd looked around at the child shouting at him. The boy was about twelve and wore a faded blue cap several sizes too large for him.

"No crazier than most," he retorted.

"Then why are you talking to yourself?"

"I'm not," Floyd said. "I'm talking to the cat."

The kid folded his arms smugly. "I don't see any cat," he said.

Floyd looked down at his feet and saw bare ground.

"Faithless creature," he muttered.

"Are you looking for someone?" the kid asked, coming over.

"Actually," Floyd said, "I'm just wondering if you've seen any monsters lately."

"You really are a crazy person," the boy accused.

"No," Floyd said, trying to be logical. "I'm trying to find a monster. He's as tall as a house, green..." he trailed off, noticing the kid's skeptical expression.

"Never mind," he said, narrowing his eyes. "I'll find him myself."

·········

"What are you doing here?" Adams asked in annoyance. "I thought I gave you a job to do."

"I'm doing it," Floyd defended himself. "Honestly. It's just..."

"What?"

"I need more data," Floyd blurted out.

Adams rubbed his hand over his face. "What more can you possibly want?" he asked wearily.

"Everything," Floyd said. "I'm trying to make a map."

"A map?" Adams repeated incredulously.

"Of the monster's movements," Floyd said eagerly, anxious to please. "I'm trying to predict his next move."

"He's a mindless beast," Adams said. "How can you predict anything like that?"

"I'm not sure it's mindless." Floyd said. "It's too..." he trailed off. "I don't know," he said. "It's a hunch, okay?"

"And I'm supposed to release confidential files so you can follow a hunch?" Adams said.

Floyd sighed. "No," he admitted.

"That's right," Adams told him. "And if I catch you in here again you are going to jail."

"I believe you," Floyd said fervently. "But Joseph..."

"Don't," the sergeant snapped. "Just don't. I'm beginning to doubt that there's even a supervillain here at all."

"I've shown you—" Floyd started, only to be interrupted again.

"What you've shown me is circumstantial at best," Adams retorted. "It looks like smoke and shadows to me. I don't want to see you until you've got something tangible, understand?"

"Like what?" Floyd demanded.

"Like a photograph of the monster," Adams tossed back. "Preferably in the act of killing a public figure."

"Like that's going to happen," Floyd muttered.

"Make it happen," Adams snapped.

"You sound like my boss!" Floyd protested.

"I am your boss," Adams said, raising his eyebrows. "At least until you prove you're not a terrorist. So get to work."

"I'm no terrorist!" Floyd exclaimed.

"Evidence," Adams said, waggling his fingers. "Go get it."

Muttering under his breath, Floyd went.

....

Floyd's flat was messier than ever. The table had been cleared of it's useless load, but the entire heap of old papers had been dumped on the kitchen floor, making it almost impossible to reach anything in the room without slipping on the whole mess. The entire living room was hung with maps and papers and diagrams, most of them incomprehensible as a result of the number of times they'd been changed.

Floyd paced among them, changing things here and there, pinning up new pictures and taking others down. He flopped on the sofa to survey his work, but he still didn't like what he saw. Whatever the monster was up to, it didn't make sense. It didn't make sense because it should have been random, and it wasn't.

He got up and sat at the table where his laptop was plugged in. Adams wouldn't give him anymore information but there was still the entire Internet. Surely someone had seen something, mentioned something...

The world was ablaze with news of the supervillains, but none of it was any help whatsoever. No one was talking about a green-skinned monster the size of a house staging a political coup.

His subconscious choice of words made him pause. What if the incidents weren't random? What if the data was right? What if there was a pattern—a reason the politician had died? What if he had been meant to die on the bridge that night? What if the entire incident had been engineered by... by...

By a mastermind. A monster alone could never work logically, methodically. He was driven by his emotions—rage, greed, and desire for disorder and chaos. He couldn't control himself. But by using mind-control or drugs a mastermind could order his comings and goings. He could direct him to a specific target and call him back again. A mastermind could harness the chaotic energy of a rampaging monster and use it as an unstoppable weapon.

With startling rapidity, the pieces fell into place. If a mastermind were behind it all, then it explained everything. The lack of supervillains. The lack of information. The seemingly random targeted deaths. Feverish with excitement, Floyd entered new search criteria, looking for any other important figures who had died since the supervillain outbreak began. The results justified his suspicions. Floyd laughed with delight. He finally had evidence.

·········

When Sergeant Adams' phone rang in in the middle of the night it was usually an emergency, so he bolted upright and answered as alertly and intelligently as he could.

"Joseph?" said the irritatingly familiar voice on the other end. "This is Floyd."

"How did you get this number?"

"The clerk on duty was a very nice girl."

You could hear the smile in his voice.

"And you lied to her," Adams growled.

"Of course. But she was very nice about it."

Adams sighed. "I'm going to give you some very simple instructions," he said. "I want you to follow them to the letter. First: I am going to hang up the phone. Second: you are not going to call back. Third: you are going to forget this number. Fourth: you will never call this number again. Do I make myself clear?"

"Perfectly," Floyd said cheerfully. "But I have some important information for you first."

"Floyd!" Adams exclaimed. "It's four in the morning!"

"I know," Floyd said. "Now listen. There's more than one villain."

"This is about supervillains?"

"Of course it's about supervillains. I wouldn't wake you up to talk about the weather, would I?"

"I don't know," Adams retorted. "Would you?"

"Not unless it was malevolent weather," Floyd replied. "Now are you done attempting to throw verbal barbs at me and listen?"

"This had better be good," Adams said threateningly.

"There is more than one villain," Floyd repeated himself. "In fact, there's just as many supervillains in London as there are anywhere else in the world."

"But?" Adams said wearily, embracing the inevitable.

"But they're all in hiding," Floyd explained. "They're operating covertly under the direction of a mastermind."

"A what?"

"A mastermind is a villain with more intelligence than the average superhuman. He possesses some kind of planning or logistical abilities that give him foresight into the future, and an understanding of his underlings. This allows him to control other superhumans that may be equal or even superior to him in powers."

"You sound like you're quoting from a textbook."

"A very astute observation."

"So we have one of these mastermind people in the city?"

"Villain," Floyd corrected. "Yes. He's been deliberately deceiving us into thinking there are no supervillains for sinister purposes of his own."

"What purpose?"

"I have no idea. But I intend to find out."

"And how do you plan to do that?"

"That's where you come in," Floyd said, and again you could hear the grin. "I've figured out who his next target is."

"Wait—target?"

"Yes," Floyd said patiently. "I can explain about that later, all right? I've planned the route the monster is going to take and I'm going to intercept him. I need you to meet me there."

Adams rubbed his eyes. "Floyd," he said. "You're chasing shadows."

"Fine," Floyd said, his voice reflecting irritation. "Don't meet me there."

"What are you going to do?"

"I'm going to get some pictures of a giant green monster," Floyd snapped.

"Floyd, wait—"

Floyd hung up.

Adams sighed, got dressed, and went to the station.

When he arrived, the clerk was engaged in arguing with a person on the other end of the phone about how she was very sorry, but the police simply couldn't investigate every unfounded allegation of a supervillain attack.

"What's going on?" Adams interrupted.

"Just a moment," the clerk said, covering the receiver with her hand. "There's a woman on the phone complaining about a monster disturbing the peace," she explained to Adams. "She's probably drunk—"

Adams snatched the phone away.

"Excuse me, where did you say you were located?" he asked the caller.

"Right," he scribbled down the address. "We'll be right there. Thanks for calling."

The clerk stared.

"Floyd was right," Adams snapped cryptically. "Dispatch everyone you can get to that location. He was right..."

46

THE GIANT GREEN MONSTER

Floyd was quivering with excitement. From his hiding place on top of an unsuspecting civilian's roof, he watched the street below, camera in hand.

It was a quarter after four and the street was still and empty. A chain-link fence ran around some corporate property on one side, and tenant houses crowded together on the other. A flickering yellow street light cast a pale glow on the sidewalk. Most of the windows were dark.

It was freezing cold, but the reporter didn't seem to mind. He was scarcely even breathing, his attention fully engaged by the absence of villainy on the street below.

BANG-crumble-rattle-shake.   BANG-crumble-rattle-shake. Every footstep was like the stroke of doom. Floyd wondered how the thing had got around this long without leaving more evidence of itself behind. Surely the pavement couldn't withstand that kind of weight and power. Surely—

BANG-crumble-rattle-shake.

It was close. Very close. Floyd held his breath as the monster came into the glow of the streetlights.

It paused right in the circle of light, as though waiting to be admired. Floyd raised his camera and started snapping pictures.

It was every bit as huge as it had been described, and even more ugly. Large, calloused feet were planted firmly in the pavement, much in the way that a redwood is stuck in the ground. They were gnarled like tree bark, and a sort of yellow-green that was hard to make out in the pale lighting. The feet were attached to legs that were thick, solid, and knobby. The legs traveled up to attach to a fat torso and that stretched upward into the darkness above the street light, obscuring the creature's face. Floyd had no doubt that the rest of it was as hideous as the visible parts.

The monster continued to stand in the lamp light, snuffling about. It suddenly occurred to Floyd to be worried about what the monster was sensing. It took a deep snorting breath and let out a hideous and ear shattering roar. It bellowed into the night with a breath that rattled all the windows for a quarter mile.

The silence that followed was sudden and inexplicable. Floyd froze, but couldn't even hear the creature's ear-rattling and irregular breathing. Floyd panicked and scrabbled backwards, prepared to jump off the roof, but it was too late. One huge hand flew flew through the air and did it for him.

Floyd hit the ground and rolled, coming to his feet a few feet away from the monster. He

48

regained his balance and crossed his arms, trying to maintain some semblance of being in control of the situation.

"All right then," he said, pretending that interrogating the monster had been his plan all along. "Who do you work for?"

Slowly, like the climax in an action film, a huge, green, gnarled and horrible looking fist appeared in the lamp light, coming down towards Floyd's head. Floyd crumpled into a little ball and rolled safely away, coming to his feet at about the same time that the fist crushed the ground where he'd been standing mere seconds before.

Floyd repeated his question.

....

Before the supervillain outbreak, Johnny McGee had been an ordinary guy. He worked in a factory that made little plastic parts for some kind of device he could never remember the name of. He worked all day, slept all night, and got drunk on the weekends. He lived in a squalid flat, ate pizza three nights a week, and watched an inordinate amount of television. His favorite programs usually involved an unrealistic amount of blood and gore, and a certain percentage of people being killed in horrible and unusual methods.

He was a big man, 6'5" and weighing over three hundred pounds. He had friends, but wasn't quite sure of the exact definition of the word. To Johnny, friends were the people you got drunk with on Friday night and complained about women and taxes to. He wasn't sure he really knew the names of half the people he considered friends, and they probably didn't know his either.

He didn't read about the supervillain incident in Kansas, he heard about it on the news a month later. It didn't seem important, because it didn't come up at any time over drinks on Friday night. Later that week he heard someone mention it at work, but he rarely paid attention to the things people mentioned at work.

He didn't notice when he started gaining weight. He didn't even notice that he was eating more than usual. When he started growing he didn't notice that either. It wasn't until he started sleeping for days at a time and got fired from his job at the factory, subsequently running out of money to pay for food and shelter, that he actually sat up and realized what was going on.

He didn't like it. His skin had taken on a greenish tinge, and moving seemed like a heavy burden. He wanted to express his unhappiness to someone, but he didn't really have anyone he could talk to seriously, and anyway, he didn't feel like moving. So he did what most unhappy people do: he screamed his frustration to the sky.

The sound of his voice startled him into silence for almost a whole day. It was so loud, so powerful, so intimidating. That was when he realized that he had changed—that he had become powerful and intimidating. This new sense of power appealed to him. He tried standing up straight for the first time in his life and discovered that he was now almost as tall as most of the buildings around him. He gave an experimental swing at one of them, and discovered that his fist went straight through it without hardly feeling it. Delighted at this discovery, he laughed aloud, and set out to cause chaos and mayhem.

His rampage had hardly started when it was abruptly halted. Before he knew what was happening, the slow, sluggish feeling had returned. He went where he was told and did what he was told, exactly as he had when he was working at the factory. He answered to a boss. He didn't like taking orders, and had a vague feeling that he shouldn't have to, but thinking made him tired, and the boss fed him, so he didn't try to do anything about it.

On this particular night, his boss had told him that he was to go to a certain place and smash it. Completely smash it. All to smithereens. This prospect had made him very happy, and so he set out. There was only one stipulation, the boss had said. He wasn't to smash anything else along the way. This made the creature that had been Johnny unhappy, but it was always better to do what the boss had said, so he had done his best to obey.

Halfway there he'd run across a couple of puny humans. They looked so tempting and delicious, but then they had disappeared. This made Johnny so angry that he completely forgot about his instructions and smashed everything in the vicinity trying to find them. Slowly every thought and every sensation had faded from his brain, and he realized he had no idea where he was or what he was doing. So he went back.

Now he had the same instructions imprinted in his mind. Go to this place and smash it. Smash nothing else along the way. But one of those puny humans had showed up again, and it was dancing about—tormenting him the way a fly torments you in the morning when you just want another ten minutes of peaceful sleep.

"Who do you work for?" the human-thing shouted. "Where are you going?"

It was using words, and giving instructions, much the way the boss gave instructions. It wasn't screaming and running the way Johnny was used to humans behaving when they saw him. It was very confusing, and he rubbed his big green head trying to sort it out.

Hitting the thing hadn't done any good. It wasn't ever where it appeared to be, or else maybe it was too small for him to smash. He wasn't sure. It was all very confusing.

"Who do you work for?" it repeated.

Johnny realized there was nothing for it but to try and come up with an answer. He tried to figure out the answer to this particular question, but he couldn't seem to think what it was. Finally he settled on the answer he usually gave when people bothered him in the pub on Friday nights.

"Go away."

His voice rumbled like the ominous tones of a severe thunderstorm, and he paused to listen to the echoes appreciatively. He forgot all about the pesky human until he realized that its squeaky voice was disturbing his reverie. Looking down he noticed it was jumping up and down and shouting. He couldn't quite make out the words, but they annoyed him all the same. He took another swing at it.

It moved out of the way again, and Johnny started to become very annoyed. He was just reaching for the lamppost when another voice broke into the human's shouting—a very familiar voice. The voice made Johnny want to relax and wait for instructions, so that's what he did. He listened very carefully to the voice, and this is what it said:

"Very well done, Mr. Floyd. Very well done indeed. It's a pity I'm going to have to kill you—and on your first assignment, too."

·········

Floyd froze in astonishment. Slowly, very slowly, he turned around. Standing behind him was a mild-looking, elderly man in a white Lab-coat. His smiling face seemed out of place compared to the shiny, very dangerous-looking gun he had in his hands.

"Put your hands up," he said. His voice made it sound like he was suggesting that if you relaxed you'd be more comfortable, but the gun suggested that if he didn't do as he was told he would end up very uncomfortable indeed. Floyd obeyed the suggestion without a quibble.

"I've been watching you, you know," the stranger said, still smiling. He might have been discussing arrangements for tea, except that he wasn't. "I've been eager to see you in action, and I must say, you do not disappoint. Your performance with the brute there—very impressive."

Floyd deemed it safe enough to venture a question of his own. "Who are you?" he asked breathlessly. "And how do you know who I am?"

"I know many things," the stranger said affably, completely ignoring his first question. "You ask too many questions."

"I'm a reporter," Floyd said. "That's what I do."

53

The stranger laughed uproariously. "I think we both know that you're not just a reporter," he said condescendingly.

"Yes, I am," Floyd said, a little too cheerfully. "I was just out taking pictures, actually. Do you want to see? My camera is... is just over there. I'll go get it."

"Don't move," the villain snapped, and Floyd decided he didn't like where this conversation was going. He decided, furthermore, that he didn't like the direction that the man in the Lab-coat was pointing his gun. In fact, he didn't like the whole situation.

"What do you want?" he asked abruptly.

"You've been working with the police, haven't you?" Lab-coat said smoothly.

"So?" Floyd demanded.

"You're far more interested in discovering the truth behind this so-called 'conspiracy theory' then actually finishing your story."

"Helping the police is how I'm going to get my story."

Lab-coat laughed again, more gently this time. "Oh, very good. Keep telling yourself that, if it makes you feel better. But now that it's begun you can't keep hiding from the truth."

"What do you want with me?" Floyd shouted.

"Oh, nothing. Nothing at all." He chuckled again. "Like I said, I'm going to have to kill you."

"You could have had the monster do that."

"Possibly. But I wanted to meet you first. Pity about the killing part. It's nothing personal, you understand. I just can't have you mucking about with my plans."

"I see," Floyd nodded. "And what plans would those be?"

"Oh, I'm afraid I can't tell you that," Lab-coat smiled.

"I see," Floyd repeated, and swallowed hard. "I don't suppose anything would change your mind about killing me?"

"No," Lab-coat said, still smiling. "I'm afraid not."

"Well," Floyd said, blinking. "I guess that's that, then."

"Yes, indeed," Lab-coat said. "Nothing personal, of course."

"Of course," Floyd said hollowly. There was a silent pause which would have been awkward if it weren't so companionable on the part of the stranger in the Lab-coat.

Floyd started, as though he'd suddenly remembered that he'd left the gas on.

"There's just one thing," he said briskly. "Something I think you've overlooked."

For the first time the stranger expressed surprise. "What would that be?" he asked.

"The policemen," Floyd said, smiling.

Lab-coat's frown deepened. "What policemen?" he demanded.

"The ones who are coming to arrest you," Floyd said.

"You're alone," the villain bellowed, but he didn't believe his own statement.

The approaching sirens became audible, and Floyd decided that now would be a very good time to run.

Two police cars careened into the alley and several things happened at once. Lab-coat shot his weird-looking gun but, since he was expecting Floyd to be running away from him, he missed. Floyd was engaged in the very odd practice of running directly towards the danger, and tackled Lab-coat to the ground. Upon seeing his master in danger the giant green monster let out a bellowing roar, then stood and waited for instructions. The police cars came to a halt, and several policemen came running towards Floyd and Lab-coat.

Adams reached them first, and pulled the villain off of Floyd. Floyd dived for the gun Lab-coat had dropped, but the villain wrenched away from the policeman and grabbed it first. The monster bellowed, the villain turned and pointed his gun at the policeman. Floyd abruptly changed direction and intercepted the trajectory of the weapon just as Lab-coat pulled the trigger.

Adams shouted. The monster roared. Floyd fell. Lab-coat dropped his gun and ran. The other policemen reached them as Adams pulled Floyd to his feet.

"You are an idiot," he said.

Floyd shook off the help and reached for the gun.

"Give me that," Adams ordered.

The monster roared one last time, then turned to follow his master.

BANG. Crumble, rattle, shake.

"Do you believe me?" Floyd asked breathlessly.

"What?" Adams said, confused. "Believe what?"

BANG. Crumble, rattle, shake.

"Please," Floyd said, grasping his shoulder. "Do you believe me?"

There was blood on his fingers, blood on his shirt.

"You're hurt," Adams said. "We have to get you to a hospital."

The monster was receding at a surprisingly rapid pace, considering his bulk.

"You saw it," Floyd repeated desperately. "You... you saw. You believe me."

"About the monster?" Adams clarified. "Yes. Yes I do. Come on, let me get you to a hospital."

"No," Floyd said, shaking his head. "No hospitals. My camera is... is behind that building."

He pointed with one shaking finger. "Get the pictures. They're the evidence you asked for."

"I don't need evidence anymore," Adams said gently. "I saw with my own eyes."

"I need help," Floyd said. "But... but first I need to go."

"Go? Go where?"

Floyd smiled in a way that very clearly indicated that he was only smiling to avoid some other expression that he very much wished to conceal.

"To the supervillain's lair, of course," and then he turned and ran.

"Floyd!" Adams shouted. "Floyd you're in no condition to—"

But he found himself shouting at an empty street, heard only by the curious ears of the other policemen. Floyd was gone.

Supervillain of the Day

THE MYSTERIOUS SECRET

Floyd woke up, blinking at the sunlight, and struggling to remember what had happened. He mentally grumbled about short term memory loss, but before he was halfway through a sensible thought it all came back in a flash. He swore violently and sat up, trying to assess the situation.

There was a hole in his shirt, and there was blood. Gingerly he took it off and inspected his shoulder where he'd been shot. It had closed up already, but it was still sore, and he gritted his teeth every time he had to move it.

Then there was Adams. Adams had been there. He knew he'd been shot. It would be impossible to explain, but he had to try, somehow. He didn't know how he was going to continue to keep secrets from the policeman once things really began.

The day kept getting worse.

Floyd stood in the middle of the room looking around at hastily scribbled notes he no longer understood. His carefully constructed

maps and probabilities had been destroyed by...
by... whatever it was he'd been doing last night.

There was a gun on the floor. It was silver
and strangely-shaped and familiar. He swept
everything off the table onto the floor and put the
gun on the newly cleared surface. One of the
papers that fluttered to his feet caught his
attention.

It was an address.

Floyd changed clothes and went on a
treasure hunt for his telephone. He dialed
Scotland Yard, staring at the silver gun all the
while.

"Sergeant Adams, please," he told the clerk.

"Hello?" Adams' gruff voice came on the line.

"This is Floyd," Floyd said, suddenly deciding
he needed to sit down for this conversation.

"Floyd," Adams said, relief evident in his
voice. "Where are you? Are you all right?"

"I'm fine," Floyd said dismissively. "I think."

The second statement had the effect of
negating the first.

"I'll come and get you," Adams said instantly.
"Where are you?"

"I'm at home," Floyd said. "Don't worry
about me."

"You were shot, Floyd!"

"That's not important."

"Not important? How is that not important?"

"Listen," Floyd said impatiently. "I can't find
my camera. Do you have it?"

"Yes," Adams said, puzzled. "You told me to
get it. Why?"

"So you have the pictures?" Floyd said
eagerly. "There are pictures, right?"

"Of the monster? Yeah. I've got them."

"Good," Floyd said in relief. "We're going to need them."

"Why?"

"As proof. To convince your superiors we're serious."

"Serious about what?"

"I have an address," Floyd said abruptly.

"An address for what?"

"For the evil lair," Floyd explained. "It's a warehouse down by the river. I followed them last night..."

"Floyd," Adams pleaded. "Will you come to the station? Please?"

"Yeah," Floyd said agreeably. "Yeah, I will. Just..."

His eyes drifted back to the gun. "Give me an hour."

"An hour?"

"I have some research to do."

"Look, whatever you want to know, we can find it out for you," Adams said. "Just come in. Please."

"See you in an hour," Floyd said, and hung up.

In a box in the bottom of his closet there was a set of fine tools he hadn't used in two years and had begun to think he would never need to use again. It took him almost half an hour to find them, and he left the room even more chaotic then it was before, but he returned to the weapon triumphant.

The next thirty minutes he spent very carefully disassembling Lab-coat's gun and inspecting every single component.

Then he called Adams back.

"Floyd?" Adams said worriedly. "Where are you? I thought you were coming in."

"I am," Floyd said. "I need you to look up every notable person who's died in London since the supervillain outbreak began, specifically politicians. Find out if there's any connection."

"Why?" Adams asked.

"Because Lab-coat has a plan," Floyd said. "And I need to know what it is."

"You have his address," Adams argued. "We don't need to understand his motives anymore."

"I have to have something to fight them with!" Floyd exclaimed. "I need to know!"

"Fight him with?" Adams said. "What are you talking about, Floyd?"

"I promise I'll explain," Floyd said softly. "Eventually. But right now I just need you to trust me."

Silence.

"I know... I know you've had your doubts about me," Floyd said hesitantly. "And I haven't exactly been honest with you. But after last night..."

"Last night you took a bullet for me," Adams said, his voice harsh to conceal his emotion. "Will you please come in so I can see for myself that you're all right?"

"I will," Floyd said, letting a smile creep into his voice. "I just need to finish things up here."

"What are you doing?" Adams exclaimed. But Floyd hung up on him again and went back to work.

Reassembling the gun went much faster then the disassembly had. When he was finished he fired it once into the ceiling to be sure it was working. It make a strange whistling sound as it discharged; quiet, efficient.

He stuck it in the pocket of his trench coat, which he then left hanging over a railing outside of the metal detectors when he went into Scotland Yard.

"Floyd!" Adams exclaimed when he saw him. "You're here!"

"Don't look so surprised," Floyd said. "I said I'd be here in an hour."

"Are you all right?" Adams pressed.

"I'm fine," Floyd brush him off.

"You're sure?"

"Of course I'm sure," Floyd said. "Did you get the information I asked for?"

"Yes, actually, I did," Adams said, trying to act casual.

"And?" Floyd asked, looking over his shoulder.

"This jumped out at me," Adams said, pulling up a news story.

"Oh, you've got a story?" Floyd said eagerly.

"I've got better than that, I've got a picture."

"They were all running for the same office?"

"Some of them were," Adams concurred.

Floyd looked at the picture and froze. "That's him," he said pointing. "Third from the right. That's the mastermind."

"The one who attacked you?"

"That's the one. He's been killing off his competition; planning to take over the city quietly. Only once his political seat is secure will he unleash his terror on the world. He's lulling us into a false sense of security so we'll never see what's coming—we won't even believe in supervillains once we're ruled by one."

Adams twisted around to stare at him.

"I'm sorry," Floyd said. "I owe you an explanation."

"Yeah, you do," Adams said, crossing his arms.

"I'm not just a reporter."

"No. You're a certifiable annoyance to law enforcement."

Floyd frowned, detecting the hostility in the policeman's voice.

"What's wrong?" he asked.

"Give me the address," Adams said.

"What?"

"The address for the lair," Adams repeated. "Give it to me, and then go home."

"I just got here."

"I know. Now I want you to give me the address and go home."

"I... I don't understand," Floyd said slowly. "Did you get the information you promised me?"

"This is dangerous work," Adams said. "You've been shot once already. I'm not letting you put yourself in danger again. Give me the address."

"No," Floyd said defiantly. "I won't deny that I'd like your help but—"

"You'd like our help?" Adams shouted. "Floyd, you're a civilian!"

"I'm also a supervillain expert," Floyd retorted.

"Supervillains didn't exist until six weeks ago. There isn't enough time to have become an expert."

"Nevertheless, I am," Floyd said. "And you'll never take out Lab-coat without me."

"Who?" Adams said, caught off-guard.

"Lab-coat," Floyd said. "The villain who shot me."

"That's what you're calling him?"

"What else am I supposed to call him?" Floyd said. "He didn't exactly introduce himself."

"That's quite possibly the worst name for a supervillain ever invented," Adams stated.

"I don't have time to come up with clever and cutesy names for these guys, okay?" Floyd exclaimed. "I just need to kill them."

"No!" Adams shouted. "No, see, that is exactly what you do not need to do."

"How are you going to stop me?" Floyd asked mockingly.

"I'll arrest you for treason," Adams threatened.

Floyd laughed.

"I can do this alone, or you can come with me," he offered. "But you're not taking me off the case."

"You don't understand," Adams protested. "This isn't even my jurisdiction. Give me the address and I'll take it to my superiors and they'll send out special forces who actually know how to deal with this."

Floyd shook his head. "I'll handle it," he insisted.

"You're going to get yourself killed!" Adams exclaimed.

"I promise I won't die," Floyd said, grinning. "Now are you coming with me?"

Adams hesitated. "I really shouldn't."

"But you will," Floyd asserted.

"I should report you."

"You won't do that."

"Don't push me."

"Come on."

"Floyd..."

He grinned. "It will be fun!"

"Floyd."

"Oh, and I want my camera back," Floyd said. "I still have that article to write."

"I thought you weren't doing it for the story!"

"I'm not! Well, I am. I have multiple motives."

Adams sighed and ran his hands over his face.

"Do you want the truth?" Floyd asked quietly.

"Of course I want the truth," Adams said, suddenly angry.

"Come with me," Floyd said earnestly. "Please."

"Is that an answer or a promise?" Adams asked.

Floyd smiled enigmatically. "Come with me and you'll find out," he said.

"You're incorrigible," Adams declared.

"That's one word for it," Floyd agreed.

"What you're doing is dangerous," Adams said, taking one last stab at warning. "Now is not the time to be a hero."

"Believe me," Floyd said in all seriousness. "Nothing could be further from my mind."

"All right," Adams said, caving in. "I'll come. But I want something in return."

"Of course," Floyd said instantly. "I promise."

"Don't promise unless you're willing to deliver," Adams warned. "I haven't said what it is yet."

"I know what you want," Floyd said. "It's a long story, and I don't know how to tell you, but when this is over.... I promise."

"All right then," Adams said, grabbing his hat and standing. "Let's go."

THE EVIL LAIR

The sun was setting when Floyd and Adams set out from Scotland Yard. Floyd retrieved his coat on the way out, Lab-coat's silver gun still safely hidden in his pocket. The wind was blowing, heralding rain to come later that night.

"I hope you know what you're doing," Adams muttered, as they hastened along in the increasing dark. Floyd didn't answer.

The dock was dark when they reached it, the last workers closing up and going home for the day. Floyd walked among the buildings, hunting for one most likely to be a lair.

"Are you sure you've got the right place?" Adams asked. "This all looks pretty harmless to me.

"Hush," Floyd admonished.

He was alert and tense, an entirely different person from the uncertain and eager reporter who'd asked for information only three days ago. He behaved like you'd expect someone to with experience in these matters to behave—like a professional. The thought made Adams more uneasy then he already was.

Floyd appeared to make his choice. Scarcely making a sound, he stepped up to the sliding door of one of the warehouses and touched it, listening.

The door opened with a metal screech that seemed too loud in the darkness, and Floyd hesitated before entering.

"It's dark," he whispered.

"Yes," Adams agreed. "That's what happens when there's no light."

"I can't see anything," Floyd protested. Their footsteps echoed in the large room as they stepped into the warehouse.

Before Adams could reply they were blinded by spotlights coming on around the room. The door slammed shut behind them. An evil laugh emanated from one end of the room, where they could just make out a shadowy figure, indistinct against the brilliant lighting.

"Welcome!" the villain said, a little too loudly. "In case you haven't noticed, you've walked right into my trap!"

"Oh, I noticed all right," Floyd retorted. "It was intentional, believe me."

"The fool-hardy reporter and the gullible policeman," the villain said. "What do I have to fear? I've been expecting you to do something stupid. Although I must say, I had rather hoped you would stay away. Wasn't almost dying once enough for you?"

Floyd shielded his eyes against the light. "Could you do a bit less with the theatrics?" he asked.

"Look around you!" The villain continued obliviously. "There is no escape."

"I'm looking," Floyd retorted. "But I can't see anything with these lights in my eyes."

"You are surrounded, outnumbered, and completely at my mercy."

"Mercy?" Floyd said incredulously. "What mercy?"

"Exactly," the villain said, going off on another of his villainous laughs.

"Are you sure you know what you're doing?" Adams asked nervously.

Floyd grinned. "Do you trust me?" he asked.

"No," Adams said shortly.

"Smart. That's very smart," Floyd said. "Keep doing that and we might even get out of here alive."

"Now," the villain said, recovering himself. "What should I do with you?"

"Oh please," Floyd said, rolling his eyes. "Like there's any doubt of that."

"You already know?" the villain expressed surprise.

"Of course I know!" Floyd retorted. "You told me the last time we met!"

"Oh yes, that's right. I almost forgot about that."

"So suppose you turn off the lights and come down here where we can converse in normal voices?" Floyd suggested.

"What makes you think we have anything to discuss?"

"Maybe the fact that we're both still talking?"

"I'm in charge here, puny human. I'll do whatever I like."

"He's trying too hard," Floyd commented to Adams. "You can tell with the way he uses completely inaccurate phrases like 'puny humans.' He's playing it completely by the book and it's coming across as shallow and cliche. Which is exactly what it is, by the way!" He shouted up to the villain. "Whoever you're taking advice from should be executed as soon as possible."

"Why should I be taking such advice from you?" the villain asked loftily.

"Because I know more about supervillains then anyone on this planet," Floyd retorted. "And the dramatic entrance went out of style before it was invented. It's just too tacky to be taken seriously anymore."

"If you were smart you would have left the country while you had the chance," the villain said threateningly.

"If I were smart I wouldn't be here in the first place," Floyd retorted. "Sorry to disappoint you."

"And what do you think you're going to do?" the villain asked. "Look around you!"

"We did this part already," Floyd snapped. "Can we get on with the action now? Please?"

"I'm sorry," Adams said, shaking his head. "But this conversation just doesn't make any sense anymore."

"As much as I'd love to try and explain it to you I'm afraid I must be going," the villain said, his voice oozing condescension.

"Oh, that's right!" Floyd said, smacking his forehead. "You have a political event tonight! Good luck with that, by the way."

"I see you figured out my evil scheme," Lab-coat said, unconcerned. "I hope I can count on your vote."

"Oh, but I almost forgot," Floyd added suddenly. "You're not going to be able to make it. What with being dead and all."

"Is that a threat?" Lab-coat said in astonishment. "Do you really think you pose any threat to me? You and your frightened police escort are powerless against my villainy."

"Frightened?" Floyd said in surprise. He glanced at Adams. "He's not frightened. You're not frightened, are you?"

"Confused would be a better word to use," Adams agreed.

"See?" Floyd said. "We're not frightened. Just very confident and—confused. Confused about things like how a dead villain can possibly run this country."

"I would advise you to watch your tongue," the villain said coldly.

"Why? Are you afraid of what I might say? Is it beginning to occur to you that I might be here for something other then just your picture? Which I can't even take, by the way, because of this terrible lighting."

"I fear nothing!" Lab-coat roared in anger. "I am a supervillain! I am the evilest villain in the world!"

"You're an amateur," Floyd retorted. "And I am not afraid of you."

"You might not want to antagonize him," Adams suggested.

"On the contrary," Floyd said. "Antagonizing is a very good idea. It unsettles him. Makes him doubt his own power."

"I doubt nothing! You will be crushed! Obliterated! Eliminated! Exterminated!"

"What, all by yourself?" Floyd said. "I very much doubt it."

"And you think you can stop me?" the villain asked again.

Floyd laughed at him.

It wasn't a cheerful laugh, or even an amused one. It was the laugh of a man who knew exactly what he was doing, or of a villain who had confidence in his ability to make an impression without theatrics. It made Adams wonder who the real mastermind in the room was, and it made the villain stare in astonishment that bordered on fear.

The floodlights shut off abruptly, leaving the warehouse illuminated with the more practical florescent lights originally installed for it. Lab-coat wasn't actually wearing a Lab-coat at all anymore. He was dressed in a business suit and looked as respectable a politician as you ever might hope to see.

"You think you're a threat?" he asked. "Let's take stock, shall we? I have at least six inches on you in height. You are unarmed. You are surrounded. I control the lights. Your backup is pathetic, weaponless, and clearly unprepared for what he is going to have to deal with. On the other hand, I have this."

He gestured dramatically and twelve doors around the warehouse slid up. Twelve henchmen walked out.

....

Blade was once a sixteen year old kid with a knife-throwing obsession. Now he was a dangerous assassin who walked around with at least thirty lethal weapons hanging from unexpected parts of his body. His hair was red with black highlights. He walked with a slump, as though relaxing against a wall that wasn't there. His pants were black and he wore something red over his chest that looked like a shirt ripped to shreds. He had an affinity for leather and spikes.

Snakeskin was twenty-three years old and engaged to be married. Her hair was black, long, and twined about her with a life of its own. Snakes wiggled from her fingertips, and sometimes emitted from other parts of her body. She had lost her ability to speak when the superpower manifested, and could only hiss, showing her pointed teeth, dripping with venom. Her eyes were narrow and unfathomable. Her clothing revealed skin that was covered with scale-like tattoos.

Brains was pale and wore huge glasses. He was dressed in a lab suit that was far too big for him and wore blue latex gloves. He could compute faster than a computer, but it was hard for him to convey his calculations, because his brain moved faster than he could talk, and his words came out in gibberish when they managed to make it to his mouth at all. He stared at the world through grey eyes that couldn't comprehend what had happened to him.

We already know about Johnny McGee, the giant green monster, so we shan't waste anymore time on him.

Slimey stood in a puddle of his own ooze. Yellow slime dripped from his finger tips, and rippled down every other visible portion of him. He wore a skin tight yellow suit, and looked distinctly and disgustingly pale, yellow and ill.

Hourglass had been a diligent watchman. He had a wife and three kids. He never told anyone about his daydreams of world dominance. He hid behind his glasses and mild mannered behavior. Now whoever he touched would die once the sand ran out through the small device that never left his hand.

Starlight was a diva, a beauty queen. She imagined herself a phenomenal success after she was hired to do a commercial for soap. Her eyes glittered enticingly, and her long blonde hair was swept up in the most flattering style. She wore a floor length, low cut gown of dark blue that revealed her smooth, perfect skin. Her fingernails were painted to match, and her entire outfit glittered with stars, but none of it matched the sparkle in her perfect eyes. Her power was that of attraction—fatal attraction. No one could resist her charms, but fell instantly under her spell once she made eye contact, leaving her free to dispose of them as she pleased.

Dotty was an elderly lady who lived in a horrid house with twenty cats. She hated people, she hated civilization, and she hated life. Now she was covered with polka dots, and anyone she came into contact with suffered from the same malady not long after.

Anatomy was a sick guy with a taste for the weird. He was living in the basement of his parents house doing things that most people prefer not to think about. He suddenly gained the ability to move his body parts at will and set out to disgust and horrify the wide open world. His hair was filthy, but under the grime it appeared to be pale in color, and he wore nothing at all.

Werewolf was pretty self explanatory. He had been a typical fantasy and goth obsessed highschool kid, and now he had morphed into an intelligent but very feral canine. He had grey fur and pointy teeth and the unsettling urge to consume human blood.

Rain Girl was followed by a perpetual thundercloud. She could control water, and dictate storms at will. She had a sunny smile, and silver hair that was strange in contrast to her young face. If you asked her why she was a villain she would sweetly and calmly tell you that humans were meant to be one with the water and she was only helping them to fulfill their destiny. It was better not to talk to her.

Gravel had been a construction worker. He didn't realize that he had any superpowers at all until an accident with a crane smashed him to bits and he stood up unharmed. He then realized that he had the ability to dissolve into gravel and reform into a human at will. He later figured out how to reform his gravel bits into boulders and various sized rocks and stones. He was invincible, unsmashable and unstoppable.

....

Floyd looked around and didn't like what he saw. He glanced at Adams, who was regarding him patiently.

"Please tell me you have a plan," Adams said flatly.

"I don't have a plan," Floyd said, near panicking.

"Then I suggest you think of a plan," Adams retorted.

"Quickly," he added, as the henchmen came closer and Lab-coat laughed.

THE DARING, IMPOSSIBLE, AND IDIOTIC PLAN

"All right!" Floyd said, stepping forward and raising his hands in the air. "Everyone stop. I don't think we've quite talked this thing through."

"There's nothing to discuss," Lab-coat said, smiling. "You are going to die, and I am going to kill you."

"That's where you're wrong," Floyd said. "First you said 'you're going to die.' For that statement to be true, you would have to have some kind of knowledge of the future, and I don't see a fortune teller among your motley band here. The second part of your statement is also false. You said 'I am going to kill you' when quite clearly you intend to stand by and watch as your henchmen kill us."

The mastermind showed his first flash of irritation. "You certainly are one for talking," he snapped.

"I haven't even got started," Floyd said, flashing a smile that served to irritate the villain further. "Now the way I see it, you've got this all wrong. You think that I'm some kind of superhero vigilante. I've got news for you. One: there's no such thing as superheroes. Two: I'm just a reporter. I only came along because my friend the sergeant here promised me a lead on a good story. I'm in the business of finding exclusive stories about supervillains, so I came along to see what all the fuss is about. Now I don't know if you've got me mixed up with someone else or what but—"

"You think that you can bluster your way out of this," the villain said. "You're wrong."

"On the contrary," Floyd said, keeping his voice honey-sweet. "I think you're going through a lot of trouble for nothing."

"What do you mean?"

"Oh," Floyd gestured vaguely. "It's all very impressive. The lights, the abandoned warehouse, the dramatic entrance—but it's also impossibly outdated. The dramatic entrance went out of style four hundred years ago. The light trick hasn't worked since they invented revolving stages. And most villains nowadays live in the lap of luxury, not derelict places like these."

"How," Lab-coat demanded, "do you know so much about villains?"

"I've been reading up," Floyd said suavely. "You don't really think you pose a threat to us, do you? I mean, sure, we're surrounded, but surrounded by what? Knife boy is only dangerous if he succeeds in hitting something. Snakelady looks horrible, but by the time she actually gets involved in the fight it will be over. And what happens if she bites herself? The anemic dweeb here should probably find a corner to hide in. We've been through what happens with the monster already. Slime is icky, but not particularly dangerous."

Lab-coat glowered but didn't interrupt. Floyd pressed rashly ahead.

"The seductress isn't going to want to get her nails dirty. Raincloud here isn't sure what to do—storms aren't very effective inside a building. Rockman is a potential problem, granted, but he's the only one so far. Werewolf is bored stiff. Cat-lady is a joke and possibly a fraud. And mister 'End of Time' looks too petrified to move his own feet. What happens if he drops that hourglass, I wonder?"

Floyd finished his analysis. "The only real threat in this room is you," he said pointedly, "and as I mentioned before, it doesn't look like you plan on doing anything."

"You underestimate me," the mastermind hissed.

"No," Floyd corrected. "You underestimate us. I mean, seriously. Why go through all this elaborate trouble? Your villains are useless to you. As high as they are on whatever mind-control drugs you're feeding them, their reactions will be sluggish at best. They're up against the finest that England has to offer, and I can tell you from experience that they don't stand a chance. We may look unarmed but we have our courage and we have our pride and we will not falter. No, my friend, there's a much easier way out of this."

"I'm listening," Lab-coat said, still annoyed.

"Like I said," Floyd repeated himself. "I'm just after the story. You can pose for a few pictures, call off your bad guys, let us walk out of here, and go on with your plans to conquer the world without the messy inconvenience of cleaning up any bodies. What do you think?"

"I don't think he would agree with you," Lab-coat said, gesturing to Adams.

Floyd shrugged. "You never know," he said. "I think I could talk him into it."

"I think that you're trying to distract me."

"It's a possibility."

"You're a smooth talker, Jeffry Floyd."

"You said that already. What is it with you and cyclic conversation?"

"Who are you, really?" Lab-coat asked suddenly. "Before I kill you I would like to satisfy my curiosity."

Floyd spread his arms out. "I am what I am," he said. "What do you make of it?"

"I'm not sure," the mastermind said with the air of a scientist. "I know a great deal about you but it doesn't all make sense. You have an air about you that is not quite human, and yet you are no supervillain."

"I wouldn't be so sure of that," Floyd said, smiling wickedly.

"A nice try," Lab-coat said, "but if you were a villain you wouldn't be working with the police."

"Perhaps they're a decoy," Floyd said. "Perhaps I just used them to get to you."

"Perhaps you're lying."

"Perhaps I'm not."

The supervillain frowned. "What are you getting at?" he demanded.

"Since I walked in through that door I've spun you six different tales," Floyd said. "You have the undesirable task of figuring out which one is true."

"Perhaps none of them are," the villain said.

"Perhaps," Floyd agreed. "Where does that leave you?"

"It leaves me back where we started," he said. "I'm going to kill you."

"Or," Floyd said, "I'm going to kill you. When you shot me last night, you left your gun behind. It's a very pretty weapon. I looked it over thoroughly."

"You're armed?" Adams said in horror and amazement.

"Get down," Floyd ordered, turned, and fired.

....

Rain Girl, Slimey, Blade, Snakeskin, Starlight, Dotty, and Brains all fell in quick succession. Werewolf and Anatomy picked themselves off the floor and started towards this new threat with alacrity. Floyd took a little more time to aim and brought down Anatomy. Werewolf was almost upon him by this time and he abandoned precision shooting in favor of simply getting out of the way.

Gravel had gathered himself up into a giant boulder and was rolling down on Floyd as quickly as possible on a level floor. He glanced up desperately at the ceiling, and at the last possible moment, jumped. Gravel smashed into Werewolf and continued onto the other side of the building, leaving behind a smear of blood and fur. Floyd fell to the floor, rolled to his feet, and brought his stolen gun to bear on the rocky heap against the wall. He fired until he ran out of projectiles and until there were more rock pieces scattered around the warehouse floor than could be reassembled in a reasonable amount of time.

The silence that followed this performance was impressive. Adams stared as the dust settled, Floyd lowered the gun slowly, and the room re-echoed with an evil laugh.

Lab-coat dusted himself off, laughing heartily and applauding with gusto.

"Very well done," he said. "Very well done indeed. But haven't you overlooked something? 'The greatest threat of them all'?"

Floyd barely spared him a glare before pointing the gun at him and firing.

Nothing happened.

Adams began to realize that something very bad was coming next.

Lab-coat kept laughing.

Floyd tried firing again, but it was useless. The gun was empty.

"You thought to lecture me on the ways of supervillains," Lab-coat said condescendingly, "But who is the naive one now? You never stood a chance. You're but a puny schoolboy in comparison to my greatness!"

Floyd didn't grace the insult with an answer.

"You did your best," the villain said, his voice adopting a consoling tone, "But I'm afraid it just wasn't enough. Now you and your useless friend will die."

Floyd tossed the gun away, prepared to take on the villain bare-handed. An ominous click made him pause.

The villain reached into his coat and pulled out another gun, identical to the one Floyd had stolen.

"It's always a good idea to keep backups," he commented, pointing it at Floyd. "And I can assure you that this one is loaded."

"Floyd, get down!" Adams shouted, distracting the villain. Floyd seized the opportunity and ran directly into the stream of bullets. The villain kept shooting, but he didn't slow down. Lab-coat started to panic just before Floyd crashed into him, knocking him to the ground.

Lab-coat hadn't been exaggerating when he said he had six inches on Floyd in height, but the smaller man fought with grace and skill that the villain could never hope to outmatch. He got control of the gun and disentangled himself from his opponent.

"You don't want to do this," Lab-coat started to protest, but before he could finish the sentence his eyes rolled back in his head and his hands went limp.

Floyd dropped the gun.

"You're an idiot," Adams said, coming up behind him. "And you're also amazing. I don't know how, and you've got a lot of explaining to do, but you did it. Floyd..."

He clapped him on the back and was slightly horrified when Floyd staggered and almost fell.

"Hey, take it easy," Adams said, grabbing his arm to steady him. "One of those bullets didn't graze you, did they?"

Floyd clung to him desperately, and Adams was horrified to see the blood splotches spreading over his shirt.

"Dear God," he whispered. "Hang on, Floyd. It will be all right. I'll—I'll call an ambulance."

"Make sure he's dead," Floyd ordered, struggling to stay on his feet. Adams spared a glance for the villain.

"He's dead," he said. "Now let's get you to a hospital."

"No," Floyd argued. "Make sure..."

He leaned down to pick up the gun he'd dropped and fell.

"Floyd, enough," Adams said forcefully.

From where he knelt on the ground Floyd managed to lift the gun and empty it into Labcoat's lifeless body.

"Burn the body," he whispered hoarsely. "All of them. Burn down... burn the whole building..."

"I'm going to call for backup," Adams said.

"No." Floyd said forcefully. "Please. Listen to me."

Unsure what to do Adams knelt beside him. "At least let me try to stop the bleeding," he said.

"It's already stopped," Floyd said. "I'm going to be fine. I'm also going to pass out. And I have to tell you first..."

"Tell me what?" Adams asked. "Floyd, you promised you wouldn't die!"

"Burn the building," Floyd repeated.

"I promise," Adams said instantly. "Now can we take you to a hospital?"

"Take me home," Floyd whispered, slumping in his arms. "It's just... it's just the regeneration taking over... promise me you won't take me to the hospital."

"Floyd," Adams said, lost for words.

"Promise..." he whispered, and that was all he managed before his eyes closed.

THE DEFENDER OF EARTH

What no one on Earth knew was that the supervillain phenomena was not, in fact, restricted to the planet, but was a particularly hard-to-remedy problem throughout the entire galaxy. It cropped up quite frequently on planets with Class III and Class IV civilizations, often as a result of experimenting with genetic alterations. One genetically altered supervillain often led to a whole outbreak of naturally altered ones, although no one had yet worked out the connection.

Methods for dealing with these supervillain outbreaks were still being explored—some with more success than others, but due to the extreme risk of one of these supervillains escaping and deciding to rule the galaxy, a strict quarantine had been imposed on any planets known to be dealing with an outbreak.

And so the galaxy was kept safe from these minor outbreaks while the greatest minds in existence worked tirelessly on finding the cause of supervillains and concocting a cure. There was known to be a standing offer of ten thousand galactic credits for any healthy supervillain who could be safely removed from the infected planet. Such specimens were transported in plastic cubes, each one certified and sealed by the quarantine division of the Galactic Police and then escorted by six battle ships to the test site. The planet-sized test site was also under quarantine and all experiments were conducted remotely using robots.

Most supervillains, once removed from their home planet, died soon after. No one is quite sure why this is, but it is firmly believed to tie directly into the cause of their existence in the first place. Those who do not die are are usually decreed artificially altered, and thus are no use to the study and promptly put to death.

The planet Earth had no idea about any of this. They believed themselves to be completely alone in the galaxy and thus completely alone with their problem. This, however, was not true.

Earth's civilization had just recently moved up from Class II to Class III in the Interstellar Transgalactic Planetary Civilization Status Index, which caused some concern in the Department of Supervillain Help and Relief Services, who were worried about Earth's lack of communication with their organization. How, they asked, would the people of Earth get through such a crisis without the help and support of their planetary neighbors? An outbreak of supervillains was a hard thing for anyone to deal with, and the transition from Class II to Class III was a very likely moment for the first outbreak to occur.

Being a very humanitarian group the DoSHRS decided that they had better do something to help in case a disaster should occur. However, because of the strict non-interference laws in first contact situations, they could not simply offer their calling card should Earth ever need their services. Neither could they turn up in the nick of time to save the world. Instead they decided to send an expert in anti-supervillain tactics to Earth to pretend he was human until such a time as he was needed.

·········

There was sunlight and there was pain. Floyd blinked against the light and winced when he sensed the pain and tried to make sense out of it all. There had been villains and police and shooting... but he appeared to be safe at home. Maybe it was all a dream. He reached out to push himself upright but snatched his hand back when he discovered that touching anything made the burning sensation worse. He couldn't place the feeling. None of it made any sense. And the thing that made the least of sense was the sound of whistling coming from the other room.

It took some time, but he grumbled and cursed his way through the process of getting washed and dressed. He stumbled out into the main room, wondering what kind of a party he'd been through and who he'd invited home with him. He stopped dead in his tracks in the doorway and had to lean on the frame for support. Staring back at him in some surprise was Sergeant Joseph Adams.

"What—" Floyd said, and stopped, surprised at how hoarse his voice sounded. He started coughing, lost his balance, and almost fell, but Adams was there in a minute.

Floyd swore; the touch of another hand on his arm was similar to heat applied to a burn. But since he hadn't sworn in English or in any language known to Planet Earth, it had no effect whatsoever on Adams. Within a few moments he was sitting on the ragged sofa and had a glass of water in his hands and managed to finish his sentence.

"What are you doing in my flat?" he demanded.

"Checking on you," Adams said simply. "You're alive, incidentally."

"Of course I'm alive," Floyd started to say, and then stopped, realizing that he had every reason not to be. He swore again.

"You're not very pleasant in the morning, are you," Adams observed.

Floyd laughed, started coughing again, and drank his water. Adams refilled his glass.

"I'm starving," Floyd observed.

"I want answers," Adams said. "Who are you?"

"The truth?" Floyd asked dully.

"That's right," Adams said, pulling up a chair.

"You won't believe me." Floyd tried to wiggle out of his promise.

"There were three holes in your chest," Adams said. "You stopped breathing for almost half an hour. And yet there you sit, alive and well, without any scars to show for it. I'll believe you."

Floyd shifted to pull his knees up to his chest and noticed that he was indeed breathing.

"3014," he said slowly. "A Class III planet called Carkbjiter experienced their first outbreak of Supervillains."

"So?" Adams asked.

"Listen," Floyd said insistently. "They'd developed the superluminal transmitter but were still working on the FTL drive. The Galactic Embassy was swamped with a political crisis between the Gassilae and the Umbra Nations and didn't have time to even file their records of the planet's first contact. Six years later, when the peace treaty had been signed and the Embassy turned their attention back to small matters like new entries into the Alliance, they were alarmed when their correspondence received no reply. Finally they sent a shuttle to investigate and do you know what they found?"

Floyd paused for dramatic effect. Adams tried to look bored—and failed.

"Everyone on the planet was dead," Floyd continued. "Most of the cities had been destroyed. A percentage of the planet no longer supported life of any kind. The landing team finally found one person who's super strength had kept him alive longer than any of the others. He told the team the team that the planet had been destroyed by supervillains. Of course it fit with what the galaxy already knew was possible with Supervillain outbreaks, but it was the worst devastation any world had ever suffered. There was a bit of a general panic in response.

"Long story short, the Department of Supervillain Help and Relief Services was founded and they later commissioned the Quarantine Division of the Galactic Police."

Floyd paused and looked up anxiously.

"Is any of this making sense to you?" he asked, slightly concerned. "You don't think I'm crazy or something, do you?"

"You're either telling the truth, you're an amazing liar, or you're totally brilliant," Adams said. "I already know you're a terrible liar and it's pretty obvious that you're not the brightest bulb in the lamp, so that only leaves one alternative. Keep talking."

"Really?" Floyd said, blinking in surprise. "That's the best you can do? I say I'm an alien and you response is that I'm not smart enough to be making it up? I have this feeling that I should be offended."

"You haven't actually said you're an alien," Adams retorted. "I'm waiting for you to get to that part."

Floyd closed his eyes.

"I was kidnapped from my homeworld," he said quietly, "and trained by the Department of Supervillain Help and Relief Services to defend this world against the supervillains, and to keep civilization alive until it develops a means of interstellar communication and establishes contact with the rest of the universe."

Adams was staggered. He knew he should say something to fit this momentous occasion, but he could only think of the obvious.

"Why aren't you dead?"

Floyd laughed, but there was no humour in it.

"Regenerative Nanobots," he said, as though it were the most ordinary thing in the world.

"What does that mean?"

"My bloodstream is full of invisible robots who zoom around patching me up whenever I get

92

hurt. It's not that complicated," he added softly. "It's nanotechnology. You're on the verge of discovering it yourselves here. Very smart people, humans. More advanced than anyone guessed."

"So you... can't die," Adams concluded.

"More or less," Floyd admitted.

The conversation died.

"So," Floyd said after a moment. "How is the world coping?"

"Not well," Adams admitted. "There was this mysterious fire down by the docks, and now all of a sudden these villains are creeping out of the shadows and annoying people. They're flighty things, and no one has quite connected it to the fire, but they're all a-flutter with speculation and disappointment."

Floyd laughed. "They'll adjust," he promised. "And I'll be out there to take care of things in a day or two."

"So what do you do exactly? Wear tights and a cape and have a secret life as a vigilante?"

"No," he chuckled. "No capes, no tights, and no secrets. I just... kill supervillains."

"Can you kill all of them?"

"No, but I can make a difference and keep them quarreling with themselves and make sure no one rises to global power."

"All by yourself?"

"I've never done this before," Floyd interrupted the interrogation. "I'll just have to see how it goes."

"And how do I fit into this?" Adams asked uneasily.

"Just... call me if you have a problem," Floyd said. "And... if I get killed, don't let them bury me. Or take me to a hospital. Or anything like that.

"And I almost forgot," he smiled. "Thank you. For saving my life. Twice."

"Well, if you can't die..." Adams said slowly.

"I can die," Floyd said earnestly. "It's just that it's rather hard to kill me."

"Thank you for helping with this," Adams said, standing up. "I should let you get your rest."

"You finally believe that I'm not a terrorist?" Floyd teased.

"You're worse," Adams retorted. "You're a spy for an alien culture. But I'll overlook it—for now."

"Thank you," Floyd repeated

"No problem," Adams assured him.

"What day is it?" Floyd asked abruptly.

Adams paused, his hand on the door knob. "Monday. Why?"

Floyd grimaced. "Deadlines," he said. "The paper went to print yesterday and I was supposed to write a supervillain story... or else."

"Does that matter now?" Adams asked in surprise. "Now that you're busy fighting supervillains?"

"Killing supervillains won't feed me," Floyd retorted.

"Well then," Adams said, reaching for something on his table. "This should reassure you."

"What?" Floyd said suspiciously.

Smiling mysteriously Adams handed him that day's copy of the London Star.

The front page featured pictures of the Giant Green Monster. The text gave a straightforward but thrilling account of the villain's secret plan to overthrow the government.

Adams laughed at the expression on Floyd's face. "I guessed something like what you told me," he explained. "So I called your office and sent this in on your behalf."

"You wrote this?" Floyd said incredulously. "And passed it off as mine?"

"Yes," Adams said.

"They believed you?"

"Any reason they shouldn't?"

Floyd met his gaze in disbelief. "I don't write this well," he said frankly. "In fact, I'm known as the worst reporter in the office."

"So now they'll have more respect for you?" Adams offered teasingly.

"Now they'll expect this every week!" Floyd retorted.

And he threw the paper across the room, smiling in spite of himself.

This is not the end.

Supervillain of the Day

ЅΝΕΑΚ PEEK

Don't miss
Supervillain of the Day: Book 2
'Fire and Ashes'
Coming February 2nd, 2013!

The flames crackled and leapt towards the sky, but as usual there was no smoke. Adams and Floyd found the fire management encampment with the emergency management, traffic management, and three fire chiefs set up already. An investigator from Scotland Yard was there, as well as half a dozen reporters.

"What have we got here?" Adams asked.

"About seventy five percent of the town is engulfed in flame," the fire chief explained. "We're doing what we can to conduct search and rescue in the remaining portions, but it's going slowly, and so far we haven't found anyone alive. There were sixty survivors who got out right away before the fire spread that far. We don't think there will be any more."

"Can I talk to them?" Floyd asked.

"I don't think they're in any condition to give their stories," a paramedic said. "We'll be sure to let you know when they can."

"All right, fine," Floyd said. "Can I get a map of the area please?"

No one answered. He looked around confused, finally glancing over his shoulder were they were all staring. The fire had died away. Instead the red-haired stranger stood alone, smiling.

Floyd swore, and walked towards the supervillain before he could change his mind.

"Hello, Floyd," Ashes said, smiling. Floyd halted a safe distance away. The villain's eyes were dancing and glowing and when he gestured sparks flew from his fingertips.

"I'm surprised to see you alive."

"Same here," Floyd said cautiously.

"I've never seen anyone survive being burned alive before."

"I've never seen anyone survive having their skull smashed in."

"I've never seen a fire damaged by a heavy pipe."

Floyd sighed. "What do you want?" he asked.

"I want to see you run," Ashes said, smiling again. "I want to see your eyes filled with fear and desperation. The end of the world is coming, Floyd. I am getting stronger. You cannot stop me, but I want to see you try."

He held out his hand and a flame sprang up out of his palm. Floyd took a step backwards.

"I've developed a distastes for hot situations," he said.

Ashes laughed. "You're afraid," he said triumphantly.

"I've got a healthy respect for pain and death," Floyd acknowledged.

"Come on," Ashes taunted. "The greatest hero in the world and you don't even want a rematch?"

"No," Floyd said. "I don't. The one thing you villains never seem to get is that I don't like confrontation. I don't like to beat you up with my bare hands. I don't like getting nearly killed, burned to death, thrown off buildings, decapitated, tortured, or any of things you seem to think I ought to enjoy."

"And yet to still try to defeat us."

"I do defeat you," Floyd asserted. "But I do it by sneaking up behind when you're not looking and hitting you on the head with a pipe. Much safer and more satisfactory all around."

"Except when your villain turns to flame," Ashes pointed out.

"Well, yes," Floyd agreed. "That was bit of a setback."

"A face to face confrontation is much more glorious," Ashes added. "Look at us now, conversing like great men from history!"

"Look," Floyd said impatiently. "There are a lot of you guys, and only one of me. I have to be as effective and efficient as possible. I don't have time for all these theatrics."

"Theatrics?" Ashes turned his hand over, as the whole thing became engulfed in flame. "Do you know what it's like to burn, Floyd?"

"Yes," Floyd said uneasily. "Thanks to you, I do."

"It's marvellous," Ashes continued, as though he hadn't heard him. "It's freedom and power. The heat and the motion... it consumes you and leaves you empty and longing for more, always, always more. And I will have it. One day, I will have it all. I will burn over the entire earth, and my glory will rival that of the sun."

"You're insane," Floyd said.

"You're afraid," Ashes countered.

"If you weren't a villain you'd be afraid too," Floyd argued.

"I can set you free," Ashes whispered. He took a step forward, more of his body turning to flame.

"No thank you," Floyd said, retreating hastily. "Some other time maybe."

Ashes laughed wildly, and suddenly burst into a column of fire that shot towards the sky.

Floyd ran.

To report a supervillain
or learn more about the series,
visit:

<u>supervillainoftheday.com</u>

A NOTE ABOUT ENGLAND

Being an American writing about England is one of the most terrifying and exhilarating things I have ever done. I've done my best to be as accurate as possible when setting this series in London, but we're all human and can make mistakes. If you're an expert or a resident of England and you find an error in this narrative, be sure to let me know about it! I'll take the correction under consideration when writing future novels, and possibly even correct the error in the omnibus version coming Summer 2013.

Submit errors using the form provided on supervillainoftheday.com and you could earn yourself a copy of the ebook version of the next novel in the series!

ABOUT THE AUTHOR

Katie is a writer of many talents, constantly branching out into new fields and genres. She primarily writes novels and short stories in the science fiction and fantasy genres, along with an assortment of hilarious and sentimental poetry. When she's not writing she's acting, directing, singing, playing her Celtic harp or songwriting, often engaging in more than one at a time. She lives in the beautiful hills of Kentucky with her parents and eight siblings.

Visit her website at katielynndaniels.com

Or follow her on twitter @danielskatie